Commander Kellie and the Superkids™

#4

In Pursuit of the Enemy

Christopher P.N. Maselli

KENNETH
COPELAND
MINISTRIES

In Pursuit of the Enemy

ISBN-10 1-57562-218-1   30-0904
ISBN-13 978-1-57562-781-6

17 16 15 14 13 12   9 8 7 6 5 4

© 1999 Kenneth Copeland Ministries

Kenneth Copeland Publications
Fort Worth, TX 76192-0001

For more information about Kenneth Copeland Ministries, visit kcm.org or call 1-800-600-7395 (U.S. only) or +1-817-852-6000.

Look for these other books in the Commander Kellie and the Superkids™ Adventure Series:

Dedication

For all the Alexes out there
who have had to face a Brock,
a Cash or even a Mashela...

Contents

Hello Superkid!

My name is Alex Taylor. In some ways, the story you're about to read isn't an easy one. Oh, sure, there's adventure, mystery and even some pretty big surprises. That comes with being a Superkid. Believe me, I know. I joined Superkid Academy four years ago and my life has been one big adventure ever since!

Just to give you a little background: Superkid Academy exists to spread the Word of God to the world...but there are those who don't want that to happen—namely, NME. NME stands for "Notoriously Malicious Enterprises" and they're always trying to destroy Superkid Academy so they can stop the message we send. Evil is like that. It never wants the Truth to be seen. Because when the Truth is shining, deception is seen for what it really is—a pack of lies.

That's why I say that in some ways, the story you're about to read isn't easy. In this one, I come face-to-face with our enemy. And they'll stop at nothing to get the upper hand. But I've learned there's something more powerful than anything the enemy can throw at you: God's Word.

With it producing love and forgiveness in your heart, your wits will be strong and the anointing God has put in you will bring you through to victory every time!

Alex

In Pursuit of the Enemy

1

Winner by Default

Shhhhhhhhhhhhhhhhh...

Alex zipped through the city on his Academy-issued, air-propelled SuperScooter. It got him where he needed to go—and quickly. Techno was strapped to the back of the vehicle that looked like a vintage motorcycle, but was made to glide above the ground in near silence.

Alex wore dark goggles that felt a tad too tight. Through them, he kept close watch on not only the road ahead, but also on the pulsating, red numbers that changed constantly, always giving him the latest coordinates of the NME Frightcraft he was tracking.

NME was bad news...literally. As a member of Superkid Academy's Blue Squad, Alex was always looking for ways to spread the Good News of Jesus, the Anointed Son of God. But NME was searching for ways to stop that news from spreading...and in its place, they strove to scatter lies, lies and more lies. Their overall mission was to get the world in the grip of fear—*their* grip of fear—so they could be in ultimate control. Meanwhile, the Superkids worked to share the message of faith in God with the world, so everyone could live free from the schemes of the devil.

The reason Alex was tracking the vehicle was because this particular craft was piloted by an NME agent Superkid Academy *had* to find. An NME agent who held a secret...and as Alex was soon to find out, she held more than one.

"Alex Taylor, you're the Superkid for the job." Those were the words Commander Kellie spoke to Alex earlier that morning.

"Me?!" Alex found it hard to stomach what his commander was suggesting. "But I'm only—I just turned 11 years old. Maybe you should send—"

"Alex, it's not your age, but the spirit inside you that counts—you can do this through the power of the anointing within you," Commander Kellie winked, quoting Philippians 4:13. Alex nodded his agreement with the Truth. If God's Word said it, he was going to believe it.

Standing in the Superkid Academy control room with Alex, Commander Kellie punched a couple buttons on a computer terminal and brought up a profile of NME agent #2039.

"Mashela Knavery," the commander voiced as the black-and-white profile buzzed down the monitor's screen. "Those close to her at NME just call her 'Shea.' She's the one who shot at Rapper and Valerie's SuperCopter from an NME Frightcraft. We need to know why."

Alex smiled and shook his finger at Commander Kellie. "Oh, I get it. You guys are trying to surprise me again, aren't you?" Just the past week, Commander

Kellie and the Superkids threw a surprise party for Alex—it was especially a surprise because Alex thought they were on an assignment. But it was a birthday party they had planned all along. "You guys are going to get me to go on a 'dangerous mission' alone and then—right when I least expect it—whammo! Happy...uh...Thanksgiving! Right?"

Commander Kellie smiled. "When was the last time you heard of a surprise Thanksgiving party, Alex?" Alex rubbed his chin with his forefinger.

"Well, since it's only September, it *would* be a surprise." Alex chuckled. OK. So he was pushing it. She was serious. "Who is it I'm tracking down again?"

"Mashela Knavery. Ever heard of her?" Commander Kellie motioned toward the monitor. Alex studied the black and white rendition of her face.

"The only Mashela Knavery I've ever heard of is the one whose middle name is 'trouble.' She's a highly decorated secret agent. A weapons specialist with covert maneuvers training—but I know you wouldn't send me alone after *her.*"

Commander Kellie just smiled. Alex felt his stomach turn.

It was no joke. Alex was the only one available for the job. The other Superkids in the Blue Squad were still on vacation. Paul and Missy had gone to Nautical, their hometown. Rapper and Valerie were on Calypso Island, finishing up their week of relaxation with Valerie's parents. But Alex was at the Academy. He was available because he had chosen to stay behind when he heard the weather on Calypso Island was forecast to be rough. Well, that and his dad had two tickets to the *Spinners'* basketball game finals. And Alex loved watching the *Spinners* play. They were incredible at basketball. Each year for the past five years, they had won the championship. He just didn't want to miss it. Now, somehow, he wished he had.

If he had missed the *Spinners'* game, he would have gone to Calypso Island for vacation. And if he had gone to Calypso Island, he wouldn't be back at Superkid Academy yet. And if he wasn't at Superkid Academy yet, he wouldn't have been commissioned to track down Mashela Knavery. And if he hadn't been commissioned to track down Miss Knavery, he wouldn't be zipping through the crisp air, wearing tight, dark goggles and watching flashing coordinates constantly remind him he was closer to finding her.

Suddenly, the red coordinates froze. She had stopped. Alex kept soaring through the air, drawing closer every moment.

"There!" Alex shouted and pointed ahead. Techno whirled his head around to look where Alex was pointing.

"Where?" Techno asked as Alex slowed down the SuperScooter. Alex looked all around the area ahead. The midday sun pierced the chilly, windy city. Alex had driven into an older section of town. The block was filled with rickety apartments and boarded-up businesses that were once the heart of a thriving metropolis. As technology advanced and business boomed, most of the companies had either prospered and moved to the north of town (the new heart of the city), or they had crumbled under the weight of competition.

"According to these coordinates," Alex said looking at the red numbers, "the Frightcraft is parked right where that old warehouse stands."

The triple-story warehouse that stood before Alex and his robotic companion looked like a skyscraper that had been pressed down into three stories. Hundreds of tiny, murky, cracked windows wrapped around the building. A thick, concrete base surrounded the structure as though it was melting. Alex imagined it had been built somewhere around the close of the 20th century. Now the cement drive leading up to a giant, solid-looking garage door had four small trees growing through it. The front door had a larger-than-life, rusted padlock dangling from the handle.

Alex smacked the coordinate computer on his air-scooter. "Thing must not be working right," he mumbled.

"There!" Techno shouted.

"Where?" Alex replied, spinning around toward his electronic friend. The shiny glass dome on Techno's head moved slightly.

"Inside. I ran a standard scan and I read one presence inside. And a large craft is there, too. Communication waves are coming from the craft. The person is talking with someone electronically."

Alex nodded. Mashela Knavery and her Frightcraft must be inside. He didn't doubt Techno's abilities. They'd been friends too long for that. Sure, Alex knew Techno was a robot, but he was also a valuable part of the Blue Squad. And over time, as Alex learned more about computers, he appreciated Techno more and more. Sure, ultimately he wasn't more than a few circuit boards and memory chips in a shiny, white, metal casing. But Techno held a massive amount of information and performed numerous electronic functions. ...And in his memory banks were the many interactions and encounters of the Superkids. He was always a clear asset to the team, and Alex considered him a friend.

Alex turned off the SuperScooter and it gently floated down to the ground and rested on its wide parking wheels. Alex unstrapped Techno from the air-scooter and rolled him out of his confines.

"Let's go check this out," he ordered.

Alex pushed the SuperScooter behind a nearby wall and locked the main control panel by entering a code into it. The bike completely shut down.

The two adventurers moved toward the warehouse, careful to stay out of the open; they didn't want NME to see them coming.

Through a broken window, Alex could hear a female's voice inside, but he couldn't make out what she was saying.

"C'mon," he coaxed Techno. They moved toward the front door. Techno had a bit of trouble over the rocks, but he managed to keep up while making only a minimal amount of noise with the rollers on the underside of his wide body.

They reached the door and Alex carefully tugged at the padlock. It was firmly attached. He looked at Techno. Without a word, the robot knew what to do. He reached forward with his metal, claw-like hand, and with a surge of electro-magnetism, the lock rolled up into the claw. Then Techno clamped down with the ends of his claw over the thick, metal latch. Alex watched as the robot's grasp became greater...and greater...until...

Snap! The latch snapped in half. Techno held one half in his claw and Alex quickly reached forward to catch the other half before it slammed against the door. Then, carefully and quietly, he pulled it out.

"Good work," he whispered, but Techno was already moving in. They pushed the door open slowly and it creaked slightly.

They froze.

They waited.

Nothing happened.

They went through this ritual 10 more times until finally the gap was large enough to allow both adventurers to pass. They sneaked into a dusty entry room and headed toward a hallway. They made it all the way through when they came upon the main warehouse floor. It was empty except for a glistening, black aircraft in the center. An NME Frightcraft.

The ship looked amazingly eerie. It was about the size of a family vehicle, with a black body and a tinted glass cockpit. The nose angled down like a vulture's beak and the three landing gears looked like crow's feet. The body itself was box-shaped, giving it the appearance of being a highly sophisticated stealth plane with the ability to transport. Nowhere on the craft was there an NME insignia, but that didn't surprise Alex. After all, it was supposed to be a secret aircraft, not an advertisement. Rumor had it there were only four of its kind in existence.

Alex and Techno could hear the female voice coming from the other side of the craft...or maybe from inside it. The back hatch was open, creating a built-in ramp. Peering underneath, they could see the door on the far side was also open to the ground. Alex signaled Techno with his hand and they made their way to the craft. Alex wanted to hear what she was saying.

They drew closer and finally they could make out her voice clearly.

"...sir, got it just where I want it."

Now Alex could hear another voice...a familiar voice... but he couldn't quite make out what it said. It kept talking and he finally recognized it. It was Major Dread—the leader of the local NME organization. *So he's the one she's in communication with,* Alex thought.

"The Disaster Virus has been injected into their computer system. Yeah...their whole network won't know a satellite signal from a pizza deliveryman. The system's memory will be fried."

The voice on the other end laughed sadistically. Alex's forehead wrinkled. *Disaster Virus? How does that tie in with her shooting at Rapper and Valerie? Or is this something new?*

"I put it in a few hours ago...yep, my best estimate is that it will take only about 72 hours for the virus to completely spread through their computer systems. They're rather large."

Whose computer systems? Alex wondered.

"Superkid Academy will cease to be a threat."

Suddenly it pieced together for Alex. Somewhere along the way, Mashela found a link to Superkid Academy's computer network...and she fed it a virus...a virus that could interfere with their mission for an indefinite amount of time. That still didn't explain why she went after Rapper and Valerie...but Alex was ready to find out.

"Oh, no, they can't hear us. We're too far away. Besides, their communication and tracking will be the first thing to go. And even if they could find us, the only Blue Squad Superkid left to send would be that Alex kid. And he's nothing to be concerned about."

Now that wasn't very nice.

"Alex."

Alex turned to Techno, who had whispered his name in a hushed shout. Alex put up his hands.

"Wait a second, buddy, I'm thinking. We have to do something. We've tracked her, but now we can't let her out of our sight. If anyone can stop the virus, she can."

"Alex," his robotic friend whirred again.

"I don't think she'll hang around here long. There's nothing here. Maybe we should call the Academy and see when someone can be here to help us."

"Alex—" Techno interrupted again.

"But if our communications are the first thing to go, it may be too late to report in," Alex thought aloud, in a whisper. "And regardless, we won't be able to track her much longer. There must be some—"

"Alex!" Techno spouted just loud enough to make Alex uncomfortable.

"Shhh! What?"

"I was hooked up to our main computer systems only three hours ago."

"So?"

"So I just scanned my systems. I have the virus, too."

2

Flight or Fight: Part I

"What are you saying?" Alex demanded, still hushed.

"I caught the Disaster Virus when I was hooked up to Superkid Academy's network this morning," Techno explained. "At least they have 72 hours to find an answer. But I'm much smaller. My system will terminate long before that!"

"Terminate? What?! You mean you only have a few hours left to live? You mean you could..." Alex couldn't say the word.

"Unless you can find a way to stop it, my memory and all functions will be—"

"Wiped out," Alex finished. "But-but you have a backup, right? We can use that."

"It's on the main system," Techno countered. "And the main system is *infected!*"

Alex's stomach felt like an avalanche of rocks had caved into it. If he didn't do something—and soon—he could lose not only Superkid Academy's main computer system, but also one of his best friends.

If the computer system at Superkid Academy went down, they would lose the ability to interrupt NME's evil broadcasts. They would lose all the technological advancements they had made to spread the Word. They would have to start over from scratch.

And if Techno went down, they'd have to start over from scratch with him, too. He would have no memory of their times together. He wouldn't know who Alex was from...well, like Mashela Knavery said, the pizza deliveryman.

Alex looked around and thought hard. Looking underneath the Frightcraft, he could see Mashela's dark boots move down the side ramp and farther down the side. She was done with her conversation and she was checking her vehicle out. The vehicle began to hum.

"I'm going aboard."

Techno's domed head swung around noticeably. "But don't you remember our mission?" Suddenly Techno's voice changed as he played back a crisp recording of Commander Kellie's directive. "Alex, I'm sending you out with Techno to track Mashela Knavery. Once you find her, stay put and we'll have reinforcements on the way to apprehend her." The recorded voice ended.

"Right." Alex wiped his forehead with the back of his hand. "But Superkid Academy's communication and tracking system could go down any moment, if it hasn't already. And Mashela's getting ready to leave again."

Techno warbled quietly.

"I have to get aboard her ship," Alex said to his computer friend. "Commander Kellie didn't know our system had a virus when she gave us those orders. I've got to think fast and this is what I need to do. We can't take the chance to go back and report in. If we do, and she leaves, we'll have lost our only opportunity to stop the virus. We need to split up. I'll stay with her and you go out and let Commander Kellie know where I am."

Techno didn't even have a chance to beep a response when they saw Mashela's shadow move back into the ship.

"Go!" Alex insisted. "Go! Before she sees you!"

Techno whirled around and rolled as quickly as he could across the smooth, warehouse floor and into the hallway they had entered moments ago. Fortunately for Techno, he was a robot and his 40 miles-per-hour rollers shot him away before the NME agent even reached the cockpit and glanced out the window. There was nothing but tiny granules of swirling dust in his path.

Alex let out a breath of relief, but his heart was still beating fast. He had to get inside the ship without Mashela noticing...and that could be tricky. She was highly trained in covert operations—which simply meant she was a specialist at hide-and-seek. Alex stole to the rear of the ship and barely had a moment to evaluate his options when the rear ramp began to rise. Instinctively, Alex threw himself inside the ship as the doors closed quickly, nearly catching his feet.

The middle of the Frightcraft, to Alex's pleasure, was packed with numerous netted, plastic cargo boxes. They blocked the cockpit from the rear of the craft, and Alex was able to duck away from Mashela's sight. He really didn't want a confrontation with her. Mashela

Knavery was thoroughly trained and an experienced NME agent. Though her file said she was only 14 years old, Alex didn't have any trouble believing her training had equipped her to outmaneuver, outwit and even out-fight any enemy she would run into.

True, Superkid Academy had prepared Alex for a myriad of situations. True, Alex was on the Blue Squad—the most prestigious squad in the Academy, with the highest-awarded commander: Commander Kellie. True, Alex had been discovering more every day who God had created him to be. But the queasiness in Alex's stomach told him he wasn't totally confident about how to handle the situation...or how to win it. The more he thought about it, he realized he hadn't thought about how he'd contact Superkid Academy later without his SuperScooter. He began to pray Techno would come through and the communication systems still worked.

Alex peeked over the boxes into the front cockpit. Foreign flight controls beeped and blinked around the pilot as she prepared the craft for takeoff. The blackness inside the craft and the blandness of the warehouse outside created a murky feeling that permeated through-out the ship.

Mashela sat in the front chair, her back to Alex. Long, curly, black hair was tied in a ponytail, neatly dangling down her back. She wore a typical, black NME pilot suit, with a hat that was a cross between a beret and the flat, old cap Alex's grandfather used to wear. Her skin was almost as dark as Alex's, and she was also wearing dark, steel sunglasses that reflected the blinking colors of the cockpit controls.

Alex wondered what to do. *What have I gotten myself into?* he thought. Then another thought struck him like a bolt of lightning in a summer storm. *He had been rushing so much, he hadn't even taken the time to ask the Lord for direction.* For all he knew, he'd just put himself in the wrong place at the wrong time. But one thing he knew for sure—it was never too late to ask.

Quietly so as not to be discovered, Alex lowered his head and gently asked the Lord for wisdom and help.

"Father God, I'm sorry for not asking You for help sooner. But I'm thankful, knowing that You forgive me for even the little things I do wrong. Now, I need Your help. We all do. Father, according to James 1:5, I ask for Your wisdom. I'm listening, Holy Spirit, for You to speak to me. In Jesus' Name, Amen."

Alex flashed back to five years ago, to when he was only 6 years old and he heard the Lord speak to him for the first time. He had been playing outside in the dirt, making castles with his brother when his dad called them in for dinner. After washing up, he sat with his family, stuffing a potato chunk in his mouth, when he heard the Holy Spirit speak to him.

Your shoes are outside, He said.

Alex looked around at the rest of his family. They were eating contentedly. His dad was talking about how he thought the *Spinners* finally had an opportunity to win their first basketball game in years. None of them had heard the voice.

Your shoes are outside.

There it was again. Alex had been reading his Bible and praying regularly, always wanting to be open to the voice of God's Spirit, though he'd never distinctly heard it. Now that he thought he did, he was surprised at how much it sounded like himself.

I'm speaking to your spirit, Alex, the Holy Spirit said. Then again, *Your shoes are outside.*

"Um, can I be excused a second, please?" Alex asked his father.

His dad nodded. "Anything wrong?"

"No, I just...I'll be right back." Alex got up and exited through the back porch door. He hopped over, barefoot, to the dirt pile he and his brother had been playing in. There, beside it, were his shoes. He had taken them off so they wouldn't get dirty. They were there, just like the Holy Spirit had said. Alex picked them up and brought them inside.

BOOOOOM!!!

The moment he closed the door, he heard a bang of thunder. Large drops of rain plopped on the dry ground, eventually turning into a rainy, windy storm.

Why had the Lord spoken to him about something so trivial? Alex knew it was because the Lord cared— those shoes would have been ruined in the storm. But it was also a way for Alex to learn to easily identify God's voice. After all, if it hadn't been God's voice,

Alex wouldn't have risked anything (except perhaps a bit of embarrassment). The Lord was teaching him. And ever since that night, Alex was sure to obey Him in even the quietest, smallest, most seemingly insignificant times. Because each time he did, Alex learned to follow the Lord better. He knew how important it was to hear God's voice.

Right now, Alex was hearing the Lord say, *Stay put.* Alex felt the vehicle lift up, giving off a rushing, whooshing sound. Then it spun around in the air. Alex peeked above the boxes again slowly, taking a look out the front windows. He expected to see Mashela opening the huge, steel door to the warehouse garage.

But she didn't. Instead, she headed straight for the closed door at maximum power.

Whhhhhhhossssssssssssshhhhhh....

Wide-eyed, Alex braced himself as they shot toward the huge, solid-steel garage door. He couldn't help but let out a scream.

"AAAAAAAUUUUUUGGGGGGGGGHHHHHHH!"

Va-ROOOOOM!

The Frightcraft blasted straight through without even a jarring of impact. Alex looked back through the rear window and saw the warehouse door growing smaller in the distance. It had only been a hologram—an illusional door. Alex had no idea NME had advanced to such a high degree in holographic technology. Alex wanted to ask questions, but before he could formulate a thought, a black-gloved fist smashed into his jaw.

WHAM! Alex reeled back and fell down onto the ground.

"So I have a visitor, do I?!"

She was standing over him, confidently and coolly, with her fists tight at her hips. Her posture dared him to get up and throw a few punches of his own. Alex was too stunned to move. He never knew anyone could hit so hard.

"Wh-who's flying?" Alex finally managed to ask. Mashela smirked and let a chuckle escape.

"I put us up high enough that no one's going to run into us. We're on a direct course for NME. You'll be lucky to see the light of day again, friend."

"I don't believe in luck. I believe in God."

"Lot of good that's done ya. Look who's standing."

Suddenly the Frightcraft hit a pocket of wind and the vehicle bumped up and down in the sky. Mashela lost her footing and slipped back, falling onto her backside. Her sunglasses popped off her face and skidded on the floor. Alex hopped up.

"Ironic, isn't it?" he asked. Quickly, he bolted for the front of the Frightcraft and glanced at the controls. It was like using a computer for the first time. He recognized the keyboard, but he wasn't sure what would happen if he pushed one of the keys.

Alex noticed a lighted panel displaying the word "AUTO" above a single green button and digital numbers. Alex punched the button, assuming it would bring them out of autopilot. The last place he wanted to go was NME HQ. He was right. Suddenly the Frightcraft slipped into a slower speed, coming out of its direct course.

The jolt knocked Mashela back—she had been working her way up to him. Alex moved his fingers along the control panel looking for any familiar-looking buttons or triggers.

He pushed one.

Va-OOOOOOOOOOMMM...

Suddenly the back hatch began to open.

"You fool!" Mashela cried. She clawed her way up behind Alex, now fighting not only the turbulence, but also the air current, which longed to sweep them both out the rear of the craft.

Mashela grabbed the back of Alex's collar and pulled. He came backward instantly. Then she punched him in the small of his back.

"Aaurgh!" Alex doubled onto his side, feeling the pain sweep through him.

Alex swept his foot sideways in defense, tripping Mashela and causing her to hit the floor again. He couldn't believe he had un-footed the expert. But he had to think fast.

Going for the main steering column, Alex increased the speed, rolling it right, and quickly felt the craft respond. Mashela tossed on the floor as the craft rolled sideways, faster and faster in the air.

Alex jumped into the pilot chair and fastened the crisscross seat belt over his body. Papers and unattached items were blowing around the craft's interior making it hard to see. Mashela stood up behind Alex, but fell back, sliding along the Frightcraft's floor. Her hat flew off and sailed out the back. Alex panicked, searching for the back door's button again. He had to get it up before she flew out. He knocked a small lever down by accident, this time disengaging the harness that held down the plastic cargo boxes. The net flew open and the boxes went flying out the back, dropping into the air and plummeting into the fields below.

Mashela grabbed the net, still attached at the front, and crawled her way along the side of the craft toward Alex. He finally found the button and hit it. Slowly, the back door began to close. But that was the least of Alex's concerns. The Frightcraft was going down. Alex grabbed the flight control again and pulled hard. The craft drew up slightly, but the downward pull was too great.

Suddenly his seat whirled around and Alex was facing backward, unable to see out the front window. Standing in front of him was Mashela, who had whirled him around in fury. For the first time he saw straight into her brown eyes. They were cold, but they were searching...Alex could tell they had stories hidden deep within. Their gaze was unbroken for only a second.

Alex fully expected to feel the brunt of her gloved fist again, but the shot never came. Instead, Mashela reached down to the chair's arm, flipped up a lid and pressed a button. A button marked "EJECT."

"Noooooooooo!" Alex cried. He lunged forward, but the seat belt caught him tightly as Mashela pressed the button. A panel above the seat shot open and the seat unlocked from the floor with a thrust.

"Jesus!" Alex screamed and the Frightcraft jolted in the air at the same moment the seat popped up. The top edge of the chair caught the roofing of the Frightcraft, crumpling the back support of the seat, jolting Alex and dropping the chair back down. A huge parachute attached to the chair blasted open inside the Frightcraft, covering the space wall-to-wall. Mashela was knocked aside by the impact and grabbed the netting again for support. In an instant, both she and Alex were pulled to the rear of the craft by force. The door had been closing, but when the bottom of Alex's chair hit it, the metal dented under the impact and the hinges to the bottom half crunched apart.

The door flew off.

Alex flew out.

Mashela flew out.

Like a couple of water skiers being dragged through the water by an uncontrolled powerboat, they both flew through the air with the unmanned Frightcraft zipping ahead of them. Alex couldn't break free of the craft; his parachute was tangled up in the pilot's controls and he was stuck in his seat belt.

Mashela, on the other hand, was dangling furiously from the net, being tossed up and down in the air. Alex looked over, wide-eyed, and watched her use all her might to crawl up the net toward the ship. She was trying to get back in and get control.

Alex looked down and saw the land below getting closer—there was no way she was going to make it. They were going to crash.

Suddenly, the land turned into water.

"Lord, You are my safety and protection—You are my safety and protection," Alex repeated Psalm 91:2 over and over, praying with every breath he could release.

Alex felt another jolt. His parachute was tearing.

Mashela pulled a pocketknife out of her boot. She flipped it open and began to cut away at the net. Square-by-square, she frantically sliced the thick net apart until she was nearly dangling by a thread. That's when it happened.

Alex's parachute tore away, tossing him straight back, still bound in the chair.

Mashela's thread ripped and she went flying down.

Still moving ahead at full power, the Frightcraft hit the large body of cold water first. The splash was surprisingly quieter than expected and it vanished in an array of foam and bubbles.

Alex hit the water next, pulled down immediately by the weight of the pilot seat he was bound in. His chest hurt from the tight belt around him, and he gasped for air just before sinking into the body of water.

He hit the lake bottom quickly—it was nearly 30 feet deep—and he worked fast to loosen his constraints. The parachute was floating down, threatening to capture him under its canopy. His ears burned from the pressure, like a vise was pressing inward on both sides of his head. Alex finally snapped the buckle open and kicked out into the dark, blue-green lake. The parachute missed him by mere inches, waving under the water like a giant squid.

Disoriented, Alex let a bubble of air out his mouth and watched which direction it floated. Alex had learned in his Superkid Academy training that because bubbles always go up, they can tell you which way is the way to the surface. He followed his bubble up to the top, feeling his lungs burning for air. Chills pierced his body from head to toe.

Moments later he broke free into the crisp air and gasped for a huge mouthful of fresh oxygen. Treading water, Alex looked around for Mashela, but didn't see her anywhere. The water left no indication of their accident other than the soft eruption of bubbles emerging from the sunken craft. *Now there are only three Frightcrafts in existence,* he thought briefly.

Looking around, Alex couldn't see a shoreline in any direction. He was stranded.

Alex continued to tread, but the nearly freezing water was quickly affecting him. He felt wide awake and extremely tired at the same time. The dark, blue-green water softly rippled around Alex, lulling him to relax. If it weren't for the unanswered questions racing through his mind, Alex might have given in quickly. Instead, he strove to focus—despite chattering teeth and numbing limbs. *Focus. Focus.*

Alex began to pray Psalm 91.

"I go to the God Most High for safety and I'll be protected by the God All-Powerful. Lord, You are my place of safety and protection. You are my God, and I trust You. You will save me from hidden traps and from deadly diseases. You will protect me like a bird spreading its wings over its young and...and..."

Alex allowed his eyelids to close for a moment...and the moment persisted...

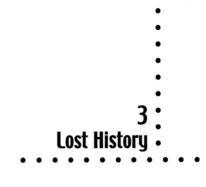

"...heart rate's increasing, doctor."
"Adjust the cardiometer reading to .55 milliamps."
"Adjusted."
"Welcome back, kid."

"...completed all minor surgery, Major. And refraction is at 100 percent and holding. Just say the word."
"Mmmmm-hmmmm. Word."
"You mean—"
"What are you waiting for? No better time than the present."

"...dosage at 80 cc. Ready for revival."
"Excellent. But let's let it take place naturally. That way we can ensure maximum results. And Professor—"
"Yes sir?"
"Don't use that word again."
"What wor—oh. Sorry. Understood."

▲   ▲   ▲

Shades of blue, yellow and white blurred into Alex's opening eyes. A large, hazy object moved back and forth about 10 feet away from him. Somehow, it was familiar...

Alex's chest felt heavy, like a stack of schoolbooks were piled upon it...and his legs felt weak, like they had fallen asleep, but the tingling had gone away long ago. He blinked his eyes tightly a couple of times, and each time he did, the blurriness lessened. The thickness in his mouth made his swallowing dry, like gulping down chocolate milk powder without adding the milk.

As the blurriness wore away, Alex relaxed as he realized he was in a familiar setting: his very own bedroom at home. Alex smiled. When he had left for his schooling and training at Superkid Academy, his mother refused to change his room even one bit. She always promised it would be ready to receive him when he came home for a visit. Alex turned his head to the left and saw his Aaron Roberts poster hanging on the wall, adjacent to the window, in the exact place he'd tacked it up five years ago. Number 23, Aaron Roberts was the *Spinners'* No. 1 player for two years in a row. Then he was out a year for a knee injury. Then he was No. 1 again for two more years. Basketball was the guy's life. Alex would have perused the poster and daydreamed longer, but light was streaming in the window, making it difficult to keep looking in that direction.

Alex raised his head. The large, blurry object moving back and forth in front of him was his mother. She was standing with her back to him, hanging some clothes up in his closet. She was just under 5½ feet tall and medium-sized. Her wavy, black hair, with streaks of gray cascading through, fell down upon her flowered, violet dress like it had for as long as Alex could remember. Nance Taylor placed security in simplicity and consistency—and you could see it in everything she did, from her clothes to her chores.

"Ma?" Alex managed to shove out. The round, dark-skinned woman made a half turn and smiled at him. "Good morning, Pumpkin," she welcomed and then twisted her arm to look at her watch. "Or afternoon I should say. You really put away the hours. Hmmm-hmmm. How you feelin'?"

Pulling his right arm out from under the comforter and blanket, Alex rubbed his eyes and wiped his forehead.

"I'm still tired," he responded. "And hot. It's so hot." Alex pushed down his blue covers, revealing his regular sleeping attire when he was at home—a gray T-shirt with small holes peppered around the collar and a pair of blue and yellow *Spinners'* shorts.

"Young man," his mother said, marching up to the side of his bed, grabbing the covers and tossing them back over him, "you may be hot, but you have to be wise. Now we're believing for this flu to leave, and while we are, I want you covered."

Alex grimaced. "Flu?"

His mother cupped her mouth with her left hand. Her wedding ring shone in the incoming light.

"Son, you don't remember the flu you came down with earlier this week? On...oh, my. It's Friday...so you came down with it on Wednesday. Mmmm. Yes, that's right, right before church."

Alex searched his thoughts, but he didn't remember having the flu...in fact, come to think of it, he didn't remember Wednesday church either. The last thing he remembered was—

"Cold water. I remember cold water."

The bed squeaked as Alex's mother gently sat down on the edge. "It's all right, Alex. It's all right. I know this must be very confusing to you, but Dr. Cole told us this could happen again. It's nothing to fear, honey. Your memory has just been affected from your accident in that Frightcraft a couple years ago. If you get sick and your defenses are down, sometimes you have a relapse, but it'll come back soon. It will."

"I...I don't understand what's happened," Alex muttered. He felt hot and tired and confused.

"Pumpkin, trust me. It'll go away soon. Just get your rest."

"I've lost my memory?" It was a rhetorical question— one that didn't need an answer, because the answer was obvious. But still it was hard to believe. Almost two years? He had that accident almost two years ago? He had always thought that when a person had a memory loss, they'd somehow know it...but then again, if they did, they wouldn't have lost their memory. It felt strange—like he'd been completely robbed of time, or transported into the future, like a couple of chapters in his life had been edited out.

"I don't understand what's happened," he said again. He could feel a lump rising up in his throat. His brain felt like a cloud had descended upon it.

Alex's mother brushed his cheek with the back of her hand. He felt her soft knuckles roll over his jawline. Alex rolled his head toward the poster on the wall.

"Where's Dad?" he asked, keeping his eyes glued to Aaron Roberts.

"He's got a flight tonight. He should be back on Sunday. Your brother and sisters are at camp." Alex blinked.

"The last thing I remember is cold water," Alex admitted again.

Using her right hand to brush the wrinkles out of the down comforter, Alex's mother carefully tried to answer Alex's questions.

"Do you remember how you got in the cold water?"

Alex thought for a second and answered, realizing the question was an easy one for him. He turned back to face his mother. Her caring eyes twinkled.

"Yeah—I remember it like it was yesterday. I was on a Superkid mission, following an NME agent. I sneaked aboard her aircraft and then...I don't know...a lot happened fast. She hit me and I fell. I remember flying out the back and that's when I hit the water."

The pause lingered.

"Then I remember landing in the middle of the lake—it was so cold. I remember cold water. And then...I don't remember anything else."

Alex's mother rubbed his shoulder. Alex reached up to feel his jaw. It felt fine. His mother looked up at the ceiling.

"Well, a lot has happened since then, Pumpkin. Oh, my, a lot indeed. Your memory should come back soon enough...but just for your peace of mind I can piece together what happened to you after you hit the lake from what Dr. Cole and Mashela said."

Alex's dark eyebrows bounced at the mention of Mashela's name.

"Mashela?" he asked. "Mashela Knavery?" Her name tasted bitter. His mother smiled contentedly.

"Yes, dear. My, this must be quite a shock for you. Well, you lost consciousness and Mashela, when she was an NME agent, she...well, she saved your life, Alex. The aircraft you went down in sent a distress signal the second it crashed and Mashela held onto you until the rescue crew came moments later."

"But why would she—"

"She's human, too, Alex. And she's changed. Hmmm. Quite a bit, I'd say. Nearly two years have passed since then. What with NME dissolved, it was easy for her to find a new life."

It was too much information at once for Alex to digest.

"Mom, I...I don't know what to think." His stomach felt queasy. It was just too much at once.

"It'll all come back to you, Pumpkin, don't worry." She smiled and tucked the comforter around Alex's neck. For a moment, she looked a bit sad. "But now you need more rest." She felt his forehead then reached over to the night stand by his bed and picked up a plastic, white thermometer. She tapped it once on his forehead, then turned it to read the instantaneous digital readout.

"One-oh-three," she said and then quoted Psalm 41:3 over him. "The Lord will give you strength when you are sick. The Lord will make you well again. Amen."

"Amen," Alex repeated.

"Well, sleep tight. I've got to go run some errands while you rest. I'll be gone for a while, but I've asked someone to come over and check up on you while I'm gone."

Alex's mom moved over and set the remaining clothes hangers in Alex's closet and then closed the closet door with a push of a button. It slid shut. Exiting the room, she tucked her clothes basket underneath her arm. She stopped at the door.

"I love you, Pumpkin."

"I love you, too, Ma."

Just as she was getting ready to push the button that closed the door, Alex asked her one final question.

"Hey, Ma? Who is it that's coming over?"

She poked her head in to the room one last time. "Someone who will take good care of you, Alex. It's your best friend, Mashela Knavery."

The door slid shut with a hiss.

Alex laid on his bed, but he did not rest.

The reality of amnesia was the strangest feeling he'd ever had. He was in the present, but to him it felt like he'd been transported into the future. A different time, a different place. Some kind of alternate reality he was mistakenly dropped into like Washington Irving's Rip van Winkle, waking up 20 years later to find that life as he'd known it had changed.

Alex reached over and slid the thermometer away from the clock display on top of his nightstand. The time was 12:38 p.m. The date was January 3. But what really surprised Alex was what the clock confirmed. It was truly a year and a half later. Last he remembered, he'd just celebrated his September 11 birthday with Commander Kellie, Paul, Missy, Rapper and Valerie— his friends at Superkid Academy. But now, according to his clock and his mom, he was almost 13—a year and a half older. He'd lost out on all that time. He sat up in bed, placed his fingertips on his forehead and concentrated. He tried to think of any memory after the crash...but none came.

"Great," he said flatly. Then he bowed his head and prayed. "Father God, I know one thing hasn't changed and that's You. Hebrews 13:8 says that You're the same yesterday, today and forever. So I pray You'll help me receive back my memory. Please help it to come back fast. I agree with 1 Corinthians 2:16 which says that I have the mind of Christ—Your anointing is with me. Father, give me wisdom, I pray."

Alex softly prayed in the spirit, lifting up his prayers in words only God could comprehend. He let the Holy Spirit pray through him and as he did, other prayers came to mind and he prayed them aloud, too.

Feeling the need to stir, Alex pushed the covers aside and slipped out of bed. He walked over to his window and looked outside. The beauty of sun-kissed snow crystals glimmered back at him, forming a soft blanket as far as Alex could see. Tree branches were bare and dark. Bushes were topped with the blanket, too. Alex still felt so warm and the room was so stuffy. He flipped the manual lock on the window and pulled. It wouldn't budge.

Great. Like his memory, it was frozen shut. Nothing seemed to be going his way. Alex moved over to his dresser and picked up the two pictures on top. One was the portrait his family had taken when Alex was born. His mom and dad looked so young and his brother was 5 and his twin sisters were 3. He was still a baby, wrapped in a blue blanket, filling the gap made for his head with puffy cheeks. Alex smiled. He glanced over at the other picture. He didn't remember when it was taken. It was him and his brother playing basketball with someone else: a girl with her back to the picture. Alex's brother had on that goofy "I'm gonna make *another* three-pointer" smile. Alex looked winded. It was a fairly recent picture by the looks of it. A time-date stamp at the bottom said, "06.07." If it was January 3, as the clock had said, the picture was only about six months old. It felt strange holding a piece of history he didn't recall. Alex put the pictures down carefully.

Alex moved over to the mirror above his desk. He pressed a contact button marked with an upside-down "V" and the mirror zoomed in to a magnified view of Alex's reflection. He studied his face. The eyelids around his brown eyes were puffy. He looked a bit flushed, but otherwise well. He looked much like he always did. It didn't surprise him that there wasn't any evidence of cuts or swelling from his battle with Mashela. It was the last thing he remembered, but it had taken place almost 16 months ago now. His face had long since healed.

The door to Alex's room suddenly slid open with a hiss. "Like I always say, 'I've never met a mirror I didn't like.'"

Alex jumped back from the mirror and nearly lost his footing. The feeling of danger rose up in his spirit. He quickly looked around for something to defend himself. His stomach rolled and his head shouted at him to do something. But there was nothing he could do. He was trapped. In the clothes he slept in.

Mashela noticed the sudden alarm on Alex's face and quickly brushed her clothes in a nervous manner. Her hair was different from when Alex last remembered her. It was prettier now—even longer and wrapped in a thick braid. She wasn't wearing the pilot uniform he remembered either. Her attire was softer—a lime-colored blouse and white skirt underneath a citrus orange and white winter coat. Her matching shoes completed the ensemble, making her appear surprisingly approachable, even for a deadly NME agent. Her eyes had lightened, too. That was what Alex had remembered most about her: the one moment he had been able to see her eyes. They had looked so hard and...sad. One glance had spoken volumes.

"Hey, Alex," she said softly, "don't be afraid. We're friends. I know that may be hard to believe, but we are..."

Alex looked at her, listening carefully. It *was* hard to believe.

"Your mom told me your memory has relapsed again. It'll come back soon, I'm sure. This happened once before, too, about four months after the accident. Your memory was back in a flash." Her red lips smiled kindly.

Carefully, Mashela took a step toward Alex. He stepped back.

"Don't be afraid, Alex. Please. Forgive me for the way you remember me. I'm a different person than I was back then. It's me—Shea. Your good friend. You really don't remember *anything* about our friendship?"

Alex hesitantly shook his head.

"I've—I've—well, look. There at that photo." She pointed to the photo Alex had just been holding, picturing him, his brother and a girl with her back to the picture. "That's me playing basketball with you and Troy. My hair's—look—" She pulled her long braid around and turned her head sideways. "It's just a little shorter in the picture than it is now. And look at my height."

Alex looked back and forth from the framed photo to Mashela. They did look remarkably similar...even if the picture was from the back.

"Do you really think your mom would allow me in your house if I wasn't your friend? If I still served *NME?*" She said the letters "NME" as though they tasted like bad milk.

"Mashela, I—"

"Call me 'Shea.'" She smiled again and bit her bottom lip.

"*Mashela.* I'm just a little edgy. I'm sorry. I really hope my memory comes back soon. I just don't understand..."—Alex waved his hands around in front of him—"...all *this.* Last thing I remember, I'm freezing in a lake—and then I wake up and my ma has me all cozy in my own bed back home. And—and—she says I've got the flu." Alex placed a hand on his stomach. "And then the one person in the past four years who tried to *kill* me is telling me she's my basketball buddy. I don't get that."

Mashela dropped her head and held her lips together tightly. A few moments of silence passed and Alex began to feel rather embarrassed for raising his voice...not to mention he was still standing there in an old T-shirt and Spinners' shorts.

When she raised her head, her eyes were watery and Alex again saw the sadness he remembered when he had first looked into her eyes. They seemed to show the door to her soul.

"I have worked so hard to gain your trust and forgiveness," she whispered, her voice quivering. "And... and now I may have to do it all over again."

"Wait a second," Alex said, quieter himself. "I thought the doctor said my memory would come back soon. This is only a relapse."

Mashela swung around, her back to Alex.

"I've said too much. I'm sorry."

"No—what? Do you know something I don't?"

Alex could tell Mashela's shoulders were tense. She was having a hard time sharing this.

"I think your mother should tell you. Not me."

"Why? What's the difference? Does Dr. Cole think this may be *more* than a relapse? Does he think this memory loss may be permanent?"

Mashela turned around and moved toward Alex. He didn't step back this time. She brushed a tear from her eye and then placed a soft hand on his shoulder.

"What's important now is that we talk about everything you can remember—especially around the time of the accident. It might be hard, but it may help your memory come back."

"Is that scientific?"

Mashela let go of his shoulder. "Alex, do you remember what happened around the time of the accident...well, I mean other than me? I can tell by your apprehension that you remember the way I used to be."

Alex wiped his forehead with his sleeve. He was still so hot.

"Do you mind if we go in the living room and talk about this?" Alex asked. "It's kind of stuffy in here."

Mashela shrugged, leading him into the adjacent room.

▲　　▲　　▲

"So where do we start?" Alex asked, his curiosity piqued. He took a seat on the familiar denim sofa. It had a soft feel, but was rugged enough for the family of six. Mashela sat beside him, turned to face him and poised herself for conversation.

"Well, you remember you boarded my ship because you were tracking me since I did that awful deed."

"You mean because you planted the virus in our computer systems or because you shot at my friends when they went on vacation?"

"Well, I know you came after me at first because I shot at..." Mashela stopped talking for a moment. Then she continued after swallowing hard. "I'm sorry... Anyway, I know why you *first* came after me. But you

boarded my ship because you found out about the virus.
Do you remember that?"

"Yeah, I overheard you so I boarded."

"Leave it to me to botch things up by talking too loud."

"And then we fought," Alex recalled, looking up
at the skylight in the ceiling. He rubbed his chin. "You
slugged me good."

Mashela smiled weakly. "Sorry."

"So my mom said you...saved me?"

"Yes, I did. The water was freezing, but I knew a
rescue craft would come soon, so I waited and kept
you afloat and I rubbed your arms to keep you warm. I
didn't think it'd be enough, but soon after our rescue, the
doctor made sure you were in good health and allowed
you to go home. You had a brief memory lapse then, but
it all came back soon enough."

"So did the virus get stopped? Is that when you
turned your life around?"

"No...it was awful what I did, Alex. It's hard to
talk about."

"Well, you don't have to if you don't want to, but I'm
kinda curious if there was even a way to stop the virus."

"Oh, there was a way, but I didn't know what it
was. Well, not exactly anyway. See, the way the virus
worked was this: First, it figured out the Main Access
Code internally. Secondly, it reversed the MAC so no
one could take control by simply putting it in like usual.
Then it wiped out the memory. So, the only way to stop it
was to program in the MAC *backward.* Then you'd gain

control and the virus would actually reverse itself and repair its damage."

"So we didn't save it?"

"No, I'm sorry, Alex. But it worked out for the best. It was when your systems went down that Superkid Academy and NME were forced to compromise."

"Compromise?" Alex didn't like the word. Mashela let it drop.

"So I'm curious," she asked, scooting closer to Alex, "what was the silly code anyway?"

Alex thought for a moment. "Well, only me and a few other people knew—you know, those of us who worked on the system the most."

Mashela listened intently.

"It was 'Alpha-four-s'—well, I guess it doesn't matter now."

Mashela sat back. They were both silent for a long moment.

"Well, Alex, I should go," she finally said, rising from her seat and stretching. "Your mom should be home soon anyway."

Alex nodded. "I can't believe I'm talking with the enemy."

Mashela glanced back and offered with a wink, "Hey now, I'm not an enemy anymore. You've forgiven me, right?"

Alex twisted his head. "Yeah, yeah. Of course, I forgive you. I'm not going to walk in darkness." Mashela blinked once in thought and Alex got up to walk her out.

"Oh, no!" she nearly shouted. "Don't get up. You need your rest and besides, you don't want to go out there."

"No, not in my shorts, Shea," Alex admitted, finally allowing himself to call Mashela by her nickname.

"Yep, it's snowy," his new friend said, folding her arms and making a fake shiver. "Brrr!"

Alex laughed for the first time since he'd awakened.

Mashela walked over to the door and then turned around to Alex one last time before she exited.

"Actually, you may not remember this," she offered, "but there's another reason you don't want to go outside. *They're* out there."

"Who?" Alex wondered. But Mashela had already left the room.

Alex got up from the denim sofa.

Who's out there? he wondered. *And why wouldn't I want to go out there if "they're" there?*

Alex made his way to the big picture window stretching along the side of the Taylor's household. Outside, the sky was cloudy and gray now, but the sun was still shining through from above. Alex didn't see any movement at all, but he could see several sets of footprints including some that looked like they had been made by a curious deer. Alex's family had always lived near Fox Trot Forest, a natural habitat for deer, raccoons and many other wildlife creatures, and the footprints had always been a welcome sight—especially for the house packed with four kids who loved to discover the world.

But Alex saw no indication whatsoever of anyone who would be a threat. No NME agents, no thieves—nobody at all! What Mashela said didn't make sense. But then again, not much of anything was making sense to Alex.

The whole world was different. The next time Mashela returned, he was going to have to get the scoop on what happened with Superkid Academy and NME Headquarters. It was hard for Alex to believe they found, to use Mashela's word, a "compromise." Honestly, Alex couldn't believe Commander Kellie or any other commander would even *consider* a compromise with the enemy, much less agree to one. And would NME agree to a compromise and then keep their word? Not the NME Alex had known. But the world was different now, nearly two years in the future.

Alex shook his head and screamed inside, *Memory come back! In Jesus' Name, come back!* But nothing new popped into his mind except the recurring fact that a year and a half of his life had passed by and he had missed it. And Mashela made it sound like Dr. Cole wasn't sure he would ever remember it. *Well, I'm glad he's helping,* Alex thought, *but God's Word is above the doctor's word...so I'm going to believe what God's Word says—and that is that I have the mind of Christ, according to 1 Corinthians 2:16.*

Alex backed away from the long window and walked across the beige rug that tingled underneath his feet. He still wasn't convinced—and if there was someone outside, he wanted to know it. Well, he did and he didn't. He wanted to know for sure whether someone harmful was there. But he was hoping there wouldn't be. After all, why would Mashela, who seemed to be so different, want to scare him? Alex crept toward the front door, and a moment later, he felt his feet hit the smooth, tiled floor. He reached for the door-opening button.

"He's just a brainy kid—we don't want him."

"Brainy kid! Brainy kid! I think you need your brain rewired! It's set to 'lame!'"

"Ha-ha! Get outta here!"

It had lasted only a few seconds, but it jolted Alex like he had just been smacked in the face by a wayward football. Alex dropped his jaw and felt a chill of fear crawl down his spine as his mouth went dry. He quickly retracted his hand and refused to open the door. He stepped backward one, two, three steps.

The distant voices sounded so spiteful, so hurting... so familiar.

If he hadn't heard them clearly with his own ears, he wouldn't have believed they were there. He hadn't heard their voices for five years—no, almost *seven* if he'd lost a year and a half. And he honestly thought he'd never hear their voices again. He had forgiven them long ago. But it had taken so long to put them out of his mind.

Brock Haney and Cash Kotter. Their names were forged in Alex's memory like words etched in cement. These were the two kids who lived down the street, who were older and always into trouble, who believed part of their mission on earth was to make Alex's life a living nightmare.

The names they'd called him. The cut-downs they'd inflicted. The rocks they'd thrown. And the one time they'd beat him up. He was bloody and black and blue and he couldn't open his left eye. That was the only time Alex ever saw his dad lose his temper.

Even though they never beat him up again, somehow matters still grew worse. They still called him names, cut him down and threw rocks. They still got other kids riled up and told them to leave him out because he was too short, not smart enough or just the wrong color. Alex had cried himself to sleep many nights, letting no one know except his pet dog, Fargo, a miniature collie, with beautiful, long, white and black hair.

Fargo had died a few years later, and along with him the daily secrets Alex had kept inside about the ways the boys treated him. Alex never told anyone all the trouble those boys caused him—now he wished he had—but now it was too late. They had moved. Besides, Alex had made it a point to forgive Brock and Cash when he first attended Superkid Academy. It was his breakthrough when he finally told someone else. He told God. He chose to finally let go and let God really heal him from the inside out. It was the most rewarding decision of his life. Forgiveness.

Yet somehow, the voices from the past struck a chord in Alex. He wasn't angry at the boys anymore—Brock and Cash had been forgiven. In fact, he had made it a point to *not* hate them. Alex knew that the Superkid Manual—God's Word—said in 1 John 2:11 that, "whoever hates his brother is in the darkness and walks around in the darkness; he does not know where he is going, because the darkness has blinded him."

Alex didn't want to walk in darkness all his life because of the wrongs they'd committed against him.

He wanted to live in the light. And to do that, he had to forgive them. *Choose* to love them. And, one night in prayer, he did. He admitted his sin of unforgiveness to God and believed God would clean his memory from the wrong they'd inflicted. Ever since then, the Holy Spirit had been working in Alex. If anything, he felt compassion for them now. And because of that, he took on a new strategy.

He prayed frequently that each one of them would meet Jesus and make Him their Lord. According to Luke 10:2, he prayed that someone who knew Jesus would come across their paths and share God's Word with them. But suddenly—for the first time since they'd moved away years ago—Alex also found himself praying for protection. Because the voices reminded him of the cruel events that always followed the taunting. He didn't want to have to face that again—pain for no reason, breaking a boy's self-confidence for play.

Alex leaned forward.

"Hey, Stupid, did you have a short-spurt? What happened to you anyway? Was God getting rid of His rejects when you were born?"

No. He wasn't going to let them get to him. He wasn't going to let their taunting lead him to sin. He wasn't going to let their words lead him to hate. He wasn't going to let it happen! Not again! He thought of 2 Corinthians 10:5—he made a decision to capture any bad thought about them he had and change it to be in obedience with Jesus and His Word. If he was tempted to hate, he would love them instead. He *would*. But Alex still didn't reach for the "Open" button again.

They were out there. Alex heard them. And he wasn't going to go out there alone.

▲　　▲　　▲

That evening, Alex received a call from his mom. She said she'd be home late; the mission center she was working at needed extra help on this cold evening. How convenient. Alex had to be alone with the troublemakers outside, now five years older and probably five years meaner.

Alex found enough food in the refrigerator for a decent dinner, but opted for a cold glass of orange juice and a bowl of Wheatsie Eatsies in cold milk instead. He really wanted to eat the Super Sugar Crispies, now with multicolored marshmallows shaped like stars, but figured with the flu he'd better not.

After dinner, Alex was feeling better and not so painfully hot. Whatever it was he had was going away, as he had prayed and believed God that it would. Sitting comfortably amongst stitched pillows on the denim couch, Alex clicked on the remote control for the television.

A couple of channels were playing sitcom reruns and a couple more sported movies that weren't good enough to make it to the big screen. Bad acting by out-of-work performers made Alex's mouth turn up at the corners. His friend Missy would have called them "major cheezers"—her term for anyone who overacted. Alex was surprised to see literally hundreds of channels available. Last he remembered, NME had the last transmitter and they dictated all programming. But not anymore. Now, all the networks were back... nonetheless, Alex brushed by most of them, looking for any hint of SKTV, the Superkids' station that frequently interrupted NME's programming, or NME-TV itself. But they didn't exist anymore. Their only existence was in Alex's memory.

Punching the "Off" button, Alex leaned back and thought about the good times he had with the Blue Squad. Commander Kellie and the Superkids—Paul, Missy, Rapper and Valerie. And Techno. They were all his friends. An idea sparked Alex's thoughts and he hopped up and moved to the slick, white ComPhone attached to the kitchen wall by the refrigerator. He punched the secret number for Superkid Academy onto the keypad, fully expecting someone at the Academy to pop up on the view screen. Instead, it flashed white and a prerecorded operator's face filled the screen.

"We're sorry. We are unable to connect to the number you have dialed. Please recheck your number and dial again. If the problem continues, please contact your local MetroCom representative for assistance. Thank you." The screen went blank.

Alex tried the number twice more and watched the prerecorded operator tell him the same thing twice more. But he didn't bother calling for assistance. He knew he had the number right. He did call the operator to see if any other number was available for Superkid Academy, but she scoffed and said, "Hadn't been one o' them fer years, boy."

In turn, Alex tried to locate each of the Superkids' home numbers. Valerie's parents lived on Calypso Island, didn't have a stable ComPhone connection and couldn't be reached. Alex couldn't find Rapper's family. And Paul was an orphan who didn't have a family residence like the others. But when he located the Ashtons in Nautical—Missy's parents—Alex had his first ray of hope.

"'Lo?" a gruff man answered. A distinguished face came up on the screen, highlighted by bushy, white eyebrows, brown eyes, a large nose and a thin, white beard descending from a receding hairline.

"Uh, hi," Alex stammered, surprised that anyone answered. "My name is Alex, and I'm wondering if Paul or Missy are available?"

There was a long pause and then the voice asked, "Is this some kind of heartless joke?"

"Wha—huh?" Alex tried to straighten out his thoughts. "No, I just wanted to see how they were doing, I'm a Sup—"

Click. The screen went blank and the connection clicked off. Alex tried calling again, but the Ashtons refused to answer. It just didn't make sense.

Alex thought about his day long and hard that evening. But the one thing he couldn't get off his mind was his new relationship with Mashela. As much as he was trying to trust her, give her the benefit of the doubt, something still gnawed at him like a beaver whittling away at a tree.

It was her eyes. They were inviting, sweet, hopeful... but sad. So sad. Alex had seen that look many times before in others—people who didn't know Jesus as their Lord. And he had seen that look in Mashela once before—before the accident. But now, nearly two years later, after Mashela had turned her life around, she *still* looked sad inside. He sensed it with his spirit. It was almost like he could sense unforgiveness in her heart. Alex wondered for the first time if she indeed had made Jesus her Lord...another question he personally had to ask her.

Alex lay down in his bed that night and fell asleep while gazing out the window and watching the wintertime stars twinkle in the deep bluish-black sky. Only once did he awaken, when he heard his mother come in after a long day out. He saw her round face peek in the door to check on him, and right after she closed it, he fell sound asleep again.

"...perfect. But you've got to get it."

"I will tomorrow. I've still got an ace up my sleeve, Major."
"You'd better. Our time is half gone."

"...refraction still at 100 percent. Couldn't be better."
"Fine work. You'll be rewarded for this, Professor."
"And I've got more ideas where this came from."

"...dosage to 80 cc's again. Weaker physically means weaker mentally."
"As you wish."

▲　　▲　　▲

The next morning when Alex awoke, he had a pounding headache and his stomach was queasy again. And he was hot. Very hot. With a weak arm, he pushed back the covers and welcomed the brush of air against his skin. Alex didn't stir for a while, he just soaked in any coolness he could. Then, finally, he slid his feet off the side of his bed and yawned like a tired cat.

He glanced at his bedside clock.

Time: 10:49. Date: January 4. Alex huffed. It hadn't been a dream. He really had lost his memory. And he hadn't gained it back overnight.

Alex stumbled to his bedroom door and opened it.

"Ma?" he shouted out, loud enough to make his hurting head regret it. "Anyone here?" No response came. Slothfully, he walked to the glass kitchen table and lifted up a small, electronic notepad sitting in the spot he usually occupied for the breakfast meal.

> Pumpkin,
>
> I'm out & about. Be sure you get plenty of rest.
>
> I'm praying for you. Never forget that.
>
> I love you, Ma

Alex hit "delete" and tossed the notepad down on the table. He felt frustrated. So he had the flu, had lost his memory, and he had to spend most of yesterday alone. Now, today would be the same. It was so unlike his family. Usually, if ever someone was sick, they would stick around and care for each other, and pray. But he wasn't going to walk in unforgiveness, Alex promised himself. People change over the years and maybe his family had, too. But that didn't make it any easier for him. Not at all.

Despite the way he felt, Alex ate a breakfast consisting of another bowl of Wheatsie Eatsies, milk and orange juice, and then he took a shower. He knew he was supposed to rest, but his mind was too busy trying to sort through the confusion. He wasn't at peace. Normally, Alex was able to rely on the peace of the Holy Spirit to show him he was in the right place at the right time. But Alex couldn't find that peace. He was feeling anxious instead, which he passed off, unconvincingly, as just a symptom of the flu.

By the time his shower was complete, Alex was not only feeling remarkably better, but he had persuaded himself that maybe everything was all right. How couldn't it be? He tried to concentrate for long periods of time and he could almost see himself playing that basketball game six months ago with Troy and Mashela...almost. But then he'd stop to look around him and everything seemed so strange.

He felt like he was in the wrong place. He wasn't supposed to be home with the flu. He was supposed to be at Superkid Academy with his friends. Alex tried dialing the Ashtons' number once again, but there was no answer.

Alex retreated back to the living room and plopped down on the denim couch and sank into it. His strength was returning. Alex began to pray.

"Holy Spirit, show me the truth," he prayed. "Clear my mind and help me get my memory back. I thank You ahead of time for answering my prayer. I know You're at work. And, Lord, as I pray, I will do as Your Word says in Mark 11:25. I stand, forgiving Mashela for the things she once did to me, and Brock and Cash...I forgive them. I forgive my ma for not staying with me today. In the big things *and* in the little things, I forgive. And as I do, I know You'll move mountains in my life. Mountain of confusion, be removed! I'm believing, Lord, You will show me the way. In Jesus' Name. Amen!"

Alex continued to pray, first in English, then in the spirit. The more he prayed, the lighter the trouble felt. His spirit was impressed with Matthew 26:41—the verse from the Superkid Manual that said to "watch and pray."

I'll do that, Alex replied to the unction within him. There was something the Lord wanted him to know...

A sudden ring of the front doorbell jolted Alex out of his time of prayer. He got up, thankful for some company, and walked to the door. He looked at the door's identificator and couldn't believe who it said it was. Quickly, he punched the "Open" button and invited his guest in.

Commander Kellie entered with a smile. Seeing her was like receiving sight of water after a walk in the desert. If anyone could help him make sense of the questions about Superkid Academy, NME, and his friends, she could.

Like Alex, she was wearing casual, everyday clothes. She wore a simple, no-frills winter coat over her jeans and a pale blue blouse. Her hair was longer than Alex remembered. But she carried the same beauty, and the same confident smile. Her hair was the same soft, brown color. Even the sweet scent of her perfume was the same. Having served on the Blue Squad under her command for the last four years of his life that he remembered, Alex's heart melted to see his familiar friend.

Without a word or a moment's hesitation, Alex threw his arms around her and held on tight. He didn't know quite why he reacted this way, but somehow she symbolized a fountain of truth in his suddenly topsy-turvy world. The hiss of the front door automatically closing was Alex's cue to let go. He fought back the flood of emotions he had accumulated the past couple days.

"It's good to see you, too, Alex," she said kindly. Then she turned. "Oh, but wait, someone else has come here with me!" She pressed the "Open" button again and the door slid open.

"Hey, I thought you were going to leave me out here in the cold!" came an electronic voice.

"Techno!" Alex cried and he ran over to give his robot buddy a hug, too. The door closed behind him and Alex dusted off Techno's dome. "You look great."

"You don't look so bad yourself!" Techno replied.

Alex cleared his throat and invited his commander and the robot to join him in the living room. After taking off her coat, Commander Kellie followed him in and sat in Alex's dad's large, brown, reclining chair, leaving it in the upright position. She cradled her coat in her lap. Techno rolled up to her side.

"So, can I get you anything?" Alex asked, sitting on the sofa. Commander Kellie shook her head. Techno's dome rolled around, surveying the house.

"I saw your mom yesterday at the shelter," the commander began. "She told me what happened. The shelter—I work there now since Superkid Academy has shut down. I'm able to help kids find homes. With Techno's database, we're able to find and help kids who are out on the streets. It's very rewarding."

Alex nodded. He didn't want to be pushy, but he had to know. "Commander Kellie, what happened? I can't remember anything. I tried calling Paul and Missy and Rapper and Val, but I couldn't find them. What's happened since that accident I had almost two years ago?"

A short pause passed and Commander Kellie brushed her long hair behind her right ear. "This would be much easier for you to accept if you remembered."

"*Everything* would be easier if I remembered," Alex replied quickly.

"Well, where should I begin?"

"Can we start with what happened after my accident, Commander? That's the last thing I remember."

The commander winked. "You can just call me 'Kellie' now, Alex. I'm no longer your commander. 'Kellie' is fine."

Alex thought about that, but responded, "You'll always be 'Commander Kellie' to me."

"You can just call me 'Techno,'" the robot interjected. They all laughed.

"All right, let's see. Well, you went after Mashela and crashed, which was almost more than I could bear after the others had gone down. But then Mashela—to all of our surprise—saved your life. Did you know she saved your life?"

"Whoa—what do you mean the others had 'gone down'?"

"Well, that was the reason you went after Mashela—because she shot the four others down when they were on their way to Calypso Island."

"You mean the *two* others," Alex corrected. "Paul and Missy changed their mind and went to Nautical instead, remember?"

Commander Kellie looked at him like what he was saying was unsettling to her, but then she suddenly recovered. "Oh, right, right. But after we lost Rapper and Valerie, that's when losing you would have been too hard to bear."

"But I thought Rapper and Valerie were all right," Alex threw back. Commander Kellie looked at him like he was from another planet. It was obviously hard for her to discuss the death threats on her Superkids.

"Oh, sure, that's what I meant," she finally said.

Alex put his hand up. "I'm sorry to bring it up. I know everything must have been tough all at once." The commander wiped her hand underneath her eye.

Alex prodded the conversation on. "So, what happened after that? After Mashela saved my life?"

"Well, the Disaster Virus she put in our computer system still ate its way all the way through...and we were left without anything whatsoever. We were just a building full of people."

"But you still had God," Alex offered.

"Yes, true. But without the technology and with NME having the upper hand, we knew we'd better find a way to stop the war—and fast—or else the Light would never overcome the darkness.

"So," Commander Kellie continued, "we did what the Bible talks about in Ephesians 6:12. We fought 'against the rulers, against the authorities, against the powers of this dark world' by making an agreement with NME. We agreed to stop working against them if they would agree to stop their operations against us. It was a long shot, but it worked. And shortly after signing our agreements, both operations shut down as promised. Today, we coexist, Light and dark. And you know what? It works pretty well together. After all, the way I see it, without the dark, no one would see the true Light."

Alex wasn't sure he totally understood everything she said, so he just smiled. "I'm so glad you're here."

"Well, I could only stop by for a minute," she admitted, "I barely have enough time to sit down, but

I'm glad I could stop by, too." She got up, threw her coat on and moved toward the door. When she reached it, she asked, "So, do you remember all the drills we used to do?" Commander Kellie leaned forward with a smile. Techno whirred. "There's a lot of them!" he said.

"Superkid Alex Taylor, what does the Superkid Manual say in Hebrews 11:1?"

"It says, 'Faith is the substance of things hoped for, the evidence of things not seen,'" Alex snapped back with a huge grin on his face. He always liked Bible drills.

"How about Psalm 23:6..."

"Uh...oh! 'Surely goodness and mercy shall follow me all the days of my life: and I will dwell in the house of the Lord for ever,'" Alex snapped back again. He hadn't lost his touch.

"And what's Superkid Academy's MAC?"

"The main access code?" Alex asked, even though he knew what she meant. She nodded. "It's funny you bring that up, because someone asked me about that yesterday."

Commander Kellie looked down at the floor. "Well, it's no secret now. We haven't needed it since everything has changed." They both nodded. "So," she asked again, "do you remember the MAC?"

"Sure," Alex confirmed. "It's 'Alpha-four-two-seven-six-zero-two-six-three-Omega.'"

Commander Kellie nodded, proud of her one-time cadet.

"It's been really good seeing you, Alex."

"Hey, you mind if Techno stays for a while? I'd like to play some electronic tic-tac-toe with him."

Commander Kellie thought for a second, then responded, "I don't see what that would hurt. Sure. I'll pick him up tomorrow afternoon at lunch."

Alex hugged his commander and she let herself out the front door. And as she said her last goodbye, Alex thought about what he had noticed when she was telling him about his recent history. It was something he hadn't ever seen before. Her eyes looked sad, too.

Alex was lying back on his bed. The more he thought about it, the less he liked the uncomfortable feeling he was getting from every minute that passed. And it wasn't just a light feeling. Alex felt it in his spirit. As if God was trying to show him something. Something that was wrong.

Alex turned to look at Techno. The robot was staying quiet while Alex prayed and sought God for an answer.

"Techno, what's going on buddy? This is getting more confusing to me by the minute. It doesn't add up. When I wake up, I'm almost two years in the future, my archenemy is my friend, Superkid Academy has made a deal with NME and no longer exists, and all my friends from the Blue Squad are..." Alex's thoughts trickled off.

Then a thought struck him.

"Hey, Techno, how did you get rid of that virus?"

The robot whirred and warbled a beep. "What virus?"

"The Disaster Virus—the one that affected Superkid Academy's main computer systems...*and* you."

"I have no record of having a virus."

▲   ▲   ▲

Alex had dialed his mom's work number, but no one answered. For the second night in a row, Alex was mysteriously left alone. He ate some quick-mix macaroni and cheese for dinner and went to bed early. Techno powered down at his bedside.

About 11 p.m., Alex saw his mother check on him and then leave contentedly. But when she exited the room, Alex hopped out of bed—still fully clothed—and peeked out his door. He saw her round form move around the room, straightening things up, and then walk out the front door again.

Alex glanced over at the clock. 11:06. *Where's she going at this hour?* he wondered. Softly, he moved out of the bedroom and into the living room. Everything was quiet and dark. Slowly, he made his way to the front window. It occurred to him that his mother could simply be getting something out of her hovercar or checking the mail. He crouched down in front of the window and peeked out.

The snow was still glistening in the moonlight. The front yard still contained evidence of curious forest animals. But the driveway was clear. Not only of a hovercar, but also of any landing marks. That was strange. It was almost as if she hadn't even come home...

Alex dug through the hall closet and found his old, academy-issued winter coat. It was royal blue, matching his squad's deep color, with braided gold stripes rolling down the arms. He threw it on and felt his body warm to the fabric.

"Where are you going?" Techno asked. Alex's heart skipped a beat as he whirled around and saw his robotic friend standing in the doorway. Alex let out a long, hard breath.

"I was just going to get a breath of fresh air," Alex said.

"I'll go power down again then," Techno promised.

Alex nodded. "Good idea." Techno rolled back around and exited. Alex moved to his doorway and double-checked on the robot. Techno had done just what he said he would. He powered down beside Alex's bed again.

Alex closed the door and made his way to the front. He grabbed his shoes sitting by the couch and shoved them on in a flash. Then he walked to the front door. He had to investigate. His mother was out there somewhere.

Alex grabbed the doorknob.

"Brainy kid! Brainy kid! What a loser!"

"I'll make you smart! Want a rock?"

Alex let go. They were still out there. Even at the late hour. Fear tried to run up Alex's spine again.

"I've forgiven them!" Alex said aloud to no one in particular. "I've forgiven them by faith!" He reached for the knob again. No matter what his feelings were telling him, he refused to give in to the hate.

"C'mon, ugly, we won't hurt 'cha! C'mon!"

The taunting bit straight to Alex's bone. But he wasn't going to allow fear to keep him imprisoned..."God has not given me a spirit of fear, but of power and love and self-discipline!" Alex said boldly. He grabbed the doorknob.

"Brainy kid! Brainy kid!"

He pulled the door open with his eyes closed. He felt the outside air hit him and he realized he'd never breathed a breath of fresh, outside air since he'd first awakened a day and a half ago. He was waiting for a rock to come and hit him right in the head. But then he encountered the most peculiar thing: Warm, stale air was coming through the doorway instead of the crisp, winter freshness he'd expected.

Alex opened his eyes.

It was dark, but not dark with glittering snow under a glimmering moon and wild animal tracks pressed in the snow. It was more like the darkness of standing inside a building. Alex allowed a moment for his eyes to focus and the shock to wear off. He slowly unzipped his coat. He wouldn't need it. He wasn't going anywhere.

The "outside" wasn't that at all...it was "inside"—he was staring at the inside of a large building with dark platforms and walkways. Red lights and warning signs. Steel bars and cement walls. And red and yellow NME insignias plastered everywhere he looked.

It was all so suddenly real to Alex. It was suddenly real that it was a fake. But not just the door. The whole house. *Everything.* A mirror of reality, but a clouded mirror. He was being held prisoner in a house that looked like his, but wasn't...by people who looked like his friends and family, but weren't. Alex didn't understand it all yet, but one thing was for sure. All that time Alex thought he had been pursuing NME's Mashela Knavery, he was wrong. The truth was, with a tight web of lies and deception, NME had been pursuing him.

"Brainy kid! Brainy kid! C'mon, kid, I dare ya!" Alex looked up and saw the speaker above the door. It was shouting out the recorded voices, no doubt triggered by his drawing near to the front door. NME was just doing what they do best—keeping people imprisoned by fear. But it hadn't worked on Alex for long. With faith, he had taken a stand against it.

Alex softly stole back into the house and closed the door. His mind shifted gears. For the first time since he awoke, Alex felt at peace. He knew trouble lay ahead, but the truth was now out. That gave Alex the upper hand.

Careful to create only as much noise as necessary, Alex took off his coat, hung it up and went back into his bedroom. It was only 11:17 p.m. and he had a lot of work to do. It wasn't over yet. He had a plan to devise.

The house was a lie, but that was good news. To Alex, that meant he hadn't been transported forward in time. He didn't have amnesia. And if NME was still real, so was Superkid Academy. And if Superkid Academy was real, so was the fact that the other Superkids were still alive...only, he had put them in danger. Alex remembered the look of alarm on the fake Commander Kellie's face when he told her Paul and Missy had gone to Nautical on the spur of the moment and weren't on the craft Mashela had shot at. NME hadn't known that. But they sure did now. Plus, it looked like NME thought they'd fatally shot down Rapper and Valerie...but now they know they hadn't.

If time in this false world had moved the same as real time, Alex figured he'd been imprisoned for about 60 hours, assuming he had been unconscious for no more than half a day from the accident. Alex twisted his lip as he thought. That left him—at most—12 hours before the virus would totally infect and destroy Superkid Academy's computer system. By now, he reasoned, Techno had probably been entirely affected and his memory erased. But if Alex could save the large system, he would save Techno's backup...and after a quick download, his robot friend would be like new.

Alex turned and looked at the TCNO unit powered down beside his bed. TCNO stood for Telecommunicable Computer and Numerical Organizer. And there were several models available from their manufacturer, Warren Technologies. "Techno," the Superkids' pet name for their TCNO robot (based on the acronym), was one of the best around. And quite frankly, it was troubling for Alex to see that another, similar unit could have fooled him so easily.

Alex shook the TCNO unit. It powered up and whirred on.

"Good morning, Alex!" it said.

"Good morning, uh, Techno," Alex responded. "Hey, I can't sleep and I'm in the mood for some technical exploring. You mind if I sharpen my skills and perform some system maintenance on you?"

The robot computed for a second and then popped open its main control panel in agreement.

"Thanks, bud," Alex said with a smile. He punched in some simple codes to begin with—codes that let him defragment the robot's information system and perform some other, routine monthly duties. But then he got a bit more advanced.

"You are very advanced in your TCNO maintenance skills," the robot responded. "Perhaps before you do more though, we should contact Commander Kellie."

Alex stopped. "Now why would we want to do that?" The robot responded with only a whistle. Alex knew it couldn't tell the truth without blowing NME's secret operation. But it didn't matter. In a moment, the robot wouldn't even know there was a secret operation. In a moment, it wouldn't know much of anything at all.

▲　　▲　　▲

Alex was almost finished with the TCNO unit when he heard a hiss come from the living room. Someone had entered the house. Alex thanked God he was working by a lamp's light instead of his overhead light which would have been easily seen creeping out beneath the door.

With amazing accuracy, Alex punched the last few codes into the TCNO unit and powered him down. Then he jumped into bed.

Alex pulled his arm back under the covers and pretended to be asleep. He could hear the footsteps approaching. Then suddenly he remembered—he had his shirt on. Not his T-shirt for sleeping, but his casual, everyday wear. In a second, Alex whipped it off, leaving his T-shirt beneath on. He stuffed his shirt underneath his pillow. The door opened.

"He's still sound asleep," a voice whispered. It was Mashela.

Alex was lying on his side. He heard someone move around behind him. Someone else moved in front of him.

"What's this?" a man's voice whispered from in front of him. Alex didn't recognize it. "You let him keep the robot?"

"Shush—you'll wake him!" Mashela responded. "Look—it doesn't matter. What good is a TCNO unit going to do him in here anyway? Besides, we got what we wanted. We got Superkid Academy's MAC."

"You've done excellent work," a deep voice sounded behind Alex. It made his heart skip a beat. Alex felt a bead of perspiration form on his forehead. The voice was that of Major Dread—NME's local leader. If he was on the case, it must be highly important. He didn't bother with the evil, day-to-day operations. He only got involved when there was real treachery involved. "Give him a drug dosage of 80 cc's one more time, Professor. We want him to think he's still got the flu tomorrow. Then he'll be easier to handle."

Alex felt a sudden pinpoint pressure and then a ping of pain in his arm. Someone had shot him with a drug. Alex wanted to cry out or even let his face flinch, but he couldn't afford to blow his cover. Somehow it didn't surprise Alex that sickness was part of their deception.

"Done," the man in front of him responded. *The "professor"...more like "mad scientist,"* Alex thought.

"Why can't I just take care of him tonight while he's asleep?" Mashela whispered harshly.

Major Dread shuffled behind Alex. "Because I want proof that this MAC truly gives access into the Superkid Academy computer network. Once we know their network has accepted it, you can do as you wish. Don't worry, Knavery. We should have our proof in less than six hours. That's when MetroCom performs their system maintenance and we'll have a few seconds of an untraced door into Superkid Academy. By 5:30 a.m. he's all yours."

5:30? But there's no way this drug will be worn off! Alex felt his body warming up. *I've got to wake up before then if I'm ever going to have a chance to leave! Holy Spirit, help me!*

The voices began to fade in and out as Alex felt the drug taking effect.

"...refraction reading?" Major Dread.

"100 percent. Still." The professor.

"They're working excellently," Mashela replied. "These holo-projectors are by far the best we've ever had at NME. They actually have this stupid kid thinking his mother and comman..."

Alex couldn't make out the next few sentences they said. His head began to pound and his body was boiling. He nearly felt like crying, but he knew no one would help. His stomach gurgled softly. He was feeling sick.

"...he get out?" The professor. Or was that Dread again?

"Not with our system at the door. Remember, fear of facing the past can keep *anyone* confined."

Anyone ruled by fear, Alex thought. *But in Jesus, I'm not just anyone...*

The door to his room hissed.

Alex sluggishly opened an eye as they left the room and he pulled his arm out of the covers. He knew he had to wake up earlier. The drug was working fast. He moved his hand over to set the alarm time on the small, night-stand alarm clock. His fingertips were feeling numb.

Got to set that alarm...

He could barely stay awake. He stretched out his hand...

Alex's eyelids were pulling down as if gravity had hold of them.

He had to change that time...

But he could barely...

    stay...

        awake...

Hisssssssssss.

From the bedroom, Alex could hear the front door slide open, sounding like a slithering snake. It was still dark outside and things were blurry to Alex. He was hot again and his stomach hurt from the drug. He could barely see his clock reading "5:30 a.m.," but it didn't matter much. Alex knew what time it was because he had an early morning visitor. A visitor who was proud to be able to prey on her prize catch.

NME figured they had what they wanted. What would they do with a measly, brainy Superkid now? Might as well dispose of him so they can tear down the fake house they built and make room for their next evil project.

Alex could hear her footsteps brushing across the living room carpet. She was making a game of it. Cat and mouse. The thought of her coming made Alex's stomach all the more queasy. In a moment she would be in the room and she would fire at him and she would feel no remorse because her heart had grown so hard. She was a product of years of NME training and she was unwilling to listen to the Truth.

She had lied to Alex. She had deceived Alex. And she would show no mercy.

Hisssssssssss.

He was hiding best as he could, peeking out, and he could see her. She was blurry, but recognizable. And it didn't surprise him. NME had sent in the fake Commander Kellie to do their dirty work. But Alex could tell the difference. The real Commander Kellie never smirked like that...like a cougar just before it pounces on its prey. Like Brock and Cash the one time they had cornered Alex—fists clenched around rocks and no one within hearing distance.

"Are you awake, Alex?" the double whispered, cold and calm. She never left the doorway. "It would do you good to come out from hiding under the covers and see the face of the one who takes your life."

"I know who you are—who you *really* are," Alex's voice came from the bed, nearly as calm as the commander's. Alex wasn't scared. He still had peace...he still had peace.

"Why do this?" Alex asked. "What's the point?"

"Oh, c'mon," she responded sharply. "Even NME knows that every single Superkid poses a threat to the darkness. Every one of them is a light—a flame that needs to be snuffed out before it catches others on fire."

"You know the Light will always overcome the darkness," Alex said. The fake Commander Kellie flinched and swallowed hard. For a moment, even though his vision was blurry, Alex saw that sadness return to her deep brown eyes. She blinked it away.

"Say your prayers, Alex Taylor," she whispered as she raised her sleek, NME FEAR pistol.

"I already have," Alex responded. A wave of heat rushed over him.

With pinpoint accuracy, the fake Commander Kellie pulled the trigger on her weapon.

A laser bolt passed through the air and bit straight into the yellow bedcovers, straight into the heart of the figure below.

Four white feathers popped out of the laser's hole and floated down.

The commander blinked. She shot three more times into the lumpy figure. Thirteen more feathers popped out and trickled through the air.

Raging, she rushed to the bedside, between Techno and the bed, and threw back the covers. Five pillows stared back at her.

"What?!" she cried.

"Surprise," Alex's voice came from behind her. She whirled around and faced the TCNO unit. Alex's voice came out of the robot again. "So, the strongman is bound."

In an instant, the TCNO unit snatched the fake commander's wrists in its metal claws and locked tight. The FEAR gun dropped to the floor.

Across the room, Alex exited the closet he'd been watching the whole scene through and walked over to the fake Commander Kellie. "Now why don't you show your true self?" he asked.

Grinding her teeth, the commander threw out a voice command. "Holo-projectors off!" Instantaneously, the hologram standing in front of Alex faded away and Mashela was standing in its place, dressed in a black, NME uniform, her wrists still bound by the TCNO unit.

"Ugh! You *stupid kid!*" she cried, yanking with her arms, trying to get free.

"Don't hurt yourself," Alex said coyly. "That unit—I call him TechToo—he only responds to *my* voice commands now. You shouldn't have left him with me. TCNO units are my specialty. And he recorded my voice nicely, don't you think?"

Mashela let out another growl of frustration. "It doesn't matter now anyway. We have Superkid Academy's MAC. Major Dread has already put it in and it has been accepted by your system. That means that in no time, NME will reverse the Disaster Virus and be solely in control of Superkid Academy's systems. We may not know where they're located, but we'll still be able to use them."

"I don't think so," Alex replied calmly. He was suddenly feeling much better. "You see, the code I gave you wasn't the MAC, as in *Main Access Code*. It was the MAC, as in *Main Alert Code*. So, as we speak, Major Dread is alerting Superkid Academy to my whereabouts."

Mashela was so angry she was perspiring. "You won't get away with this, Alex Taylor. Remember— you're still in the center of NME Headquarters. It's a long way out."

Alex led the TCNO unit to the door, pulling Mashela
along. "Not the way we're going," he promised. "I found
a map of NME HQ inside TechToo. To my surprise,
right next door to Research and Development—where
we are—is the Vehicle Repair Center. I also found out he
has record of a waterlogged NME Frightcraft sitting in
there, just ready to bust out of this building. With only
four in existence, NME just couldn't let it go that easily,
could they?"

After punching the button, the front door slid open
with a hiss and Alex carefully looked outside.

"Brainy kid! Brainy kid!"

"Come any closer and get ready to rock!"

Mashela looked hopeful, counting on the voices
from Alex's past to surprise him, jolt him into fear. Alex
looked at her eye-to-eye and said, "God's perfect love
casts away fear." It was enough of an explanation for
Mashela to understand. Her eyes turned sad again for a
split second.

"What makes you so sad?" Alex had to ask. Mashela's
face instantly turned cold again.

Alex dropped the issue and looked around the
large room they were in. The grays and blacks, the steel
and metal, the grime and filth—it was all such a sharp
contrast to the house Alex had lived in for the past 65
hours. Alex already wanted to leave it.

"Which way, TechToo?"

The robot whirred. "Take a sharp right and cross the
room over to the second steel door!"

"Got it!" Together, the three turned right; Mashela did so grudgingly. Alex could see the door about 200 feet ahead. To Alex's relief, there were no guards. His guess was that the R&D area wasn't generally a security risk.

"Let's bolt!" Alex shouted and took off across the floor. TechToo followed him closely, careful not to move faster than Mashela could keep up. He was still holding her wrists in his clamps.

Halfway across, Alex looked up to see a large booth suspended in the air, off to the left. Inside it, he could see a large figure, which he immediately recognized as Major Dread, and another shadow he imagined was the professor. They were pressed up against the glass in disbelief that Alex had actually outwitted Mashela Knavery. Dread began to push buttons, most assuredly alerting security.

At once, an alarm sounded and Mashela let out a high-pitched scream for help. Alex heard footsteps echoing in the huge building. Red lights began to flash.

"Quiet!" Alex ordered as they ran.

"Look," Mashela spat. "Let me go and I'll let you go. I'll just tell Major Dread you got away."

"So you're saying if I'm willing to compromise, we can make a deal and both win?"

"That's right!" Mashela's face lit up.

"I don't deal with the enemy," Alex said flatly. "Besides, you're going to have to fly us out of here."

Alex, Mashela and TechToo reached the large, steel door marked "Vehicle Repair Center" just as a squadron of black-clothed troops with dark helmets rounded the corner.

Ka-pow! Ka-pow! Ka-pow!

Laser shots exploded against the wall and door as the trio rushed through. Alex shut the door behind him, but had nothing to block it with. He had to work fast.

The NME Vehicle Repair Center was a large room with a mammoth, steel garage door at the front and a wide, darkened skylight on the ceiling sporting the NME symbol. The lights in the room were off and only the flashing red from the alert lights showed the way. The place was vacant, given the early morning hour. About 25 banged and dented NME crafts were scattered around the room, each with a ramp at its side and grease, oil or gasoline at its base. Unlike most vehicles anymore, NME still used those powered by combustion instead of air. It made many of them speedier and far less expensive to build—but they were notably more noisy. However, their stealth units, like the NME Frightcraft, were equipped with the latest air-compression technology for quiet, sleek missions.

"There!" he shouted, pointing to the shiny, black NME Frightcraft. There was a puddle of water around the base, as though it had been brought in only within the last 24 hours—probably with little time to allow for repair. But that didn't sway Alex. "Let's go! Let's go! Let's go!"

TechToo followed close behind as they weaved their way through other vehicles. They ran up the ramp at its rear and entered. Since the back door had been torn off before their crash-landing, it was wide open.

Ka-pow! Ka-pow! Ka-pow!

Troops flooded in, twice the number that was after them only moments before. And they came from all directions. Alex ordered TechToo and Mashela to the front while he unlatched the metal ramp at the back.

Ka-pow! Ka-pow! Ka-pow!

"This isn't gonna start!" Mashela cursed.

"In Jesus' Name, it'll start!" Alex retorted.

Ka-pow! Ka-pow! Ka-pow!

"You've got to free my hands if you want me to fly it!"

"One, TechToo! Free *one* hand."

TechToo let the clamp around her left hand loose and she glared at Alex. "Why should I do *anything* you say?! In a second, you'll be captured."

Ka-pow! Ka-pow! Ka-pow!

"Because any second now, one of those bad-shot troopers is gonna hit a gasoline tank and we'll all be blown out of here! It's either that or we get out alive while we can!"

Mashela thought about it a second and realized he might be right. She reached over and punched some buttons. "Why not?" she said, looking up at the skylight. "This is one thing I've always wanted to do."

Ka-pow! Ka-pow! Ka-pow!

In an instant, with a spit, the Frightcraft powered up and lifted off the ground. Alex quickly caught onto the side door handle—he had almost fallen out the back.

Mashela worked the Frightcraft around, as it coughed some more, and aimed it upward. Mashela was working to keep her balance. The pilot seat was still missing from when she had ejected it earlier and she was bracing herself between the seat rails on the floor and TechToo's claws still firmly clamped around her wrist. The robot quickly fastened himself to the floor magnetically.

Sha-Voooooooooom! The Frightcraft lurched forward clumsily and shot up at an angle. Alex peeked around to see the huge, glass dome above them getting quickly closer. With a shout, Mashela shot them straight through the center of the gigantic NME symbol.

CRRRRRRRRAAAAASSSSSSHHHHHHHHHHHHH!!!

Bits of glass burst out around them, sending reflections of the rising, orange sun in every direction. Mashela smiled briefly. She worked to straighten them out and Alex let go only for a second to make it up to the front of the craft. He grabbed hold of another handle at the front.

"Now follow my directions," he ordered.

Mashela looked straight at Alex. "Don't you realize you've cost me my life? NME won't let me live for this! They're very unforgiving!"

"Your life can still change, Mashela! There is Someone who has *already* forgiven you!" Alex shouted above the cool, rushing air around them.

"NO! IT'S TOO LATE!" She shouted and plowed her hand straight into Alex's jaw once again. Alex stood his ground and touched his throbbing jaw with one hand, but refused to let go with the other.

The Frightcraft still rushing forward, Mashela kicked out with her right foot and pulled her free, left elbow back into the dome on top of TechToo's body. The kick smacked Alex right in the gut, bringing back the nauseous feelings he'd had only a short time ago when he had awakened. The elbow smashed through the robot's dome, crumbling it into a thousand pieces. With a scream, Mashela smashed back with her elbow again and the glass shards went flying in 100 directions. Alex closed his eyes and the glass whirled out the back of the craft. Mashela looked out the window and sent the Frightcraft at an angle, straight down.

Alex could hear them rushing closer to the earth and he looked up into Mashela's face. She was wild with anger as she confidently peered ahead. She didn't want any mercy, and she didn't want to give any mercy. Alex's ears popped with every moment that zoomed by. He had to get back in control.

Mashela kicked at Alex's hand, gripped around the handle. Pain forced Alex to let go and he went sliding forward into the front of the craft. For a second he was thankful they were going down instead of up.

One more elbow punch into TechToo short-circuited his systems and he demagnetized from the floor with a pop. Suddenly Alex heard a very familiar sound. It was the sound of a huge aircraft plummeting into a sea of water. Ten, then 20 feet went by in a second and the back instantaneously flooded with the murky water. Alex crawled/swam up and out of the craft as quickly as he could. He was almost out the back when the Frightcraft smashed against the lake's bottom with a boom. He looked behind him and saw TechToo, the TCNO robot, weighted on the floor. But that's not what truly caught his attention. What really caught his eye was the look of sadness in Mashela's eyes as she looked up at him, realizing she was still bound in TechToo's claw. She must have thought he would let go when he demagnetized, but he hadn't. And she was anchored at the bottom of the lake.

▲　　▲　　▲

The last thing Mashela remembered was the feeling of loss, of being alone, of her enemy staring down at her. She had been trained long ago to hold her breath for several minutes at a time, but in this case she didn't need to. Before her breath ran out, she felt her body grow tired. The cold water lulled her to relax. To give up. Her limbs became numb and no matter how hard she tried to focus, things grew blurrier. But there was one thing she knew for sure. She wasn't going to get a second chance.

She saw Alex staring down at her sorrowful eyes and then she allowed her eyelids to close for a moment...and she felt the air leave her lungs.

▲　　▲　　▲

"...heart rate's increasing, doctor."

"Thank God. Adjust the cardiometer reading to .55 milliamps."

"Adjusted."

"Welcome back, kid."

Alex cleared his throat as he entered the room. An Academy guard was posted at the door, but one wasn't really needed. The captive behind the light-blue, electronic field inside hadn't moved since she had been brought to the room over three hours ago. She was lying on her side, facing forward, with her legs curled up to her stomach and her arms curled under her head for support. She occupied a cot. She was kept warm through a series of electronic units placed carefully around the room, creating a favorable climate. A small, medical device beeped softly on her wrist, measuring her heartbeat and alerting the medical staff—two wings away—of any progress she made.

"Um, hope you don't mind a visitor," Alex said, his voice echoing off the walls of the gray room. He was in white pajamas under a white robe given to him by the medical staff. Mashela's attire was similar, but fluorescent orange and black for easy identification as a prisoner.

Alex could hear the round, florescent lights buzzing in the ceiling.

"Thought you'd want to know we stopped the Disaster Virus. We input the Main Access Code backward, like you said, and it worked. Took a while for it to repair itself, but it did." She didn't stir. Alex touched his warm mug of tea to his lips. But he didn't drink any.

The silence was awkward.

He shuffled his feet. "They also saved Techno. 'Course that was easy after the system was back online. All they had to do was copy over his backup files." He glanced up at Mashela's face and studied her beautiful, dark hair, tied in a rubber band at the back. "Would you believe they even saved TechToo?" Alex felt a smile come and go. "Have to replace his dome and they're going to paint him red to distinguish him from Techno. He'll work with another squad."

Alex looked down at his mug. It was painted with vibrant patterns of reds and yellows and oranges. Steam disappeared into the air.

"Guess it's a good thing that rescue unit got to us in time, huh? Or we'd have both frozen in that lake. Actually, we can thank Major Dread for that. It was the Main Alert Code he sent to Superkid Academy that got the rescue squad heading toward us in the first place."

The room began to feel like it was closing in.

"The other Superkids'll be back in a couple days. It'll be good to see them."

Alex reached down with his free hand and touched the bottom of his pajama shirt. The thread was coming unraveled. He rolled it between his forefinger and thumb.

"I, uh, I really didn't come to tell you all that."

The heater came on and reverberated softly against the ceiling, droning over the fluorescent lights and the soft beeping monitor of Mashela's heartbeat.

"I, well, I just came to tell you that I, uh, forgive you." The words appeared to fall flat in the room, against the walls, against Mashela's ears. But they were healing to Alex.

"You might find that hard to believe. But I...I do. I forgive you." Her sad, brown eyes blinked once. Alex drummed his mug with the fingers curled around it and he smiled softly.

Mashela's face was blank.

Alex stood silent for a long moment and then turned around on his heel.

▲   ▲   ▲

The cot she was lying on was comfortable, but the longer she lay, the harder it felt. As Alex left the room quietly, Mashela Knavery moved her eyes to watch him exit. The haze of the light-blue, electronic force field gave Alex the appearance of being a hologram.

She had heard everything Alex said and she accepted that she had been wrong about one thing: For some reason she couldn't figure out, she *was* given a second chance at life—one she didn't deserve. As she lay, for the first time since she could remember, a tear formed at the corner of her eye. She rolled her head back and let it fall back inside. She swallowed hard and felt a tightening in her heart.

She didn't think she deserved that second chance. She didn't believe things should be allowed to change that easily. And she certainly didn't believe that she could be forgiven. Not ever. Not after all she had done. If Alex had had his way, she would have never seen the surface of earth again—*that* was what she believed. To Mashela Knavery, *that* would have been justice.

Little did she know that her rescuer wasn't a medical squad who happened to arrive in the nick of time. It was the one person she had punched, kicked, threatened, deceived, lied to and tried to kill for the past four days. The short, "brainy" kid she had worked the hardest to destroy, nearly gave up his last, burning breath to dive down, painstakingly free his enemy, and give her that second chance.

Alex had gone down to visit Mashela once a day for the next three days, but each time, she looked harder, colder and angrier. She refused to speak a word or look at her visitor. Each time, Alex shared the message of salvation with her, but his words fell on ears determined not to hear.

Until the other members of the Blue Squad returned from vacation, Alex used the most of his waking hours to work with Techno and TechToo. Together, the three of them toiled to ensure NME would not be able to access the Superkid computer systems again. They were sure Mashela and NME had never discovered the Academy's actual location, and they wanted to keep it that way.

Alex was feeling chipper again by the third day when his friends arrived back from their vacations. Commander Kellie and the Superkids planned a big dinner together and each of the Superkids told of their unexpected vacation adventures.

Rapper and Valerie had gone to Calypso Island for vacation, and Valerie had gotten lost. She had quite a story about how she escaped from the jungle. Paul and Missy went to Nautical, Missy's hometown, in search of Paul's parents. He had been an orphan all his life. It was pure delight to hear the truth and the treasure he discovered there.

But the excitement reached its peak when Alex told his friends his story of waking up nearly two years in the future to an altered reality—and then his daring escape to freedom.

After dinner, Paul asked if Alex would take him down to see Mashela. "I'd like to tell her about what I learned during vacation," he offered, "about the covenant God has made with us."

"She hasn't said a word for four days," Alex said.

"That's all right. I'll just count it as planting seeds of truth in her life. But I don't want to keep this revelation I received a secret."

"I want to come, too," Missy interjected. "Maybe she'll be more willing to open up if another girl's there."

Alex shrugged and took them down to her. Rapper and Valerie offered to stay behind with Commander Kellie and the robots to clean up.

When they entered the room, Paul was the last to walk in, but when he did his eyes grew wide.

"Shea?!" he shouted, staring disbelieving at the figure behind the light-blue force field. Mashela blinked, and a look of recognition washed over her face. For the first time in four days, Alex saw her move.

Imaginary question marks covered Missy's and Alex's faces as Paul moved closer.

"Shea?! Are you telling me *you're* Mashela Knavery? No way!"

Mashela brought herself to a sitting position and squinted in wonderment. "Pauly?!" she whispered.

Missy looked at Alex with a curled upper lip. "Pauly?"

Alex shrugged.

"Oh my...ha-ha!" Paul whirled around and looked at Alex and Missy. *"This* is who caused you all that trouble?" Alex nodded.

"I don't doubt it. Oh, my...ha-ha! It's so good to see you! I've heard of Mashela Knavery, but I had no idea it was you!" Paul shouted. Mashela's face grew to a wide smile. It was such a contrast to what Alex had seen that it appeared fake. Alex wondered if maybe it was.

"Paul...I can't believe it," she whispered. Paul turned to Alex and Missy again.

"This is *Shea Brown!* She lived at the orphanage with me for a couple years! I haven't seen her in *forever!"*

"Not long enough," Missy murmured.

"Wait—this is *Mashela Knavery,"* Alex corrected.

"I changed my name when I joined NME," she whispered. Then she addressed Paul. "I had no idea the kid named 'Paul' on the Blue Squad was you. You're really a Superkid?"

Paul threw out his hands. "That I am! This is great, seeing you again. We have so much catching up to do!" He clapped his hands together and laughed again. "Oh boy, I'll have to get clearance to shut off this force field."

Alex and Missy stared in disbelief.

"I don't think I like the look of this," Missy said under her breath.

Alex wiped his forehead with his hand. "You don't know the half of it."

To be continued...

Prayer for Salvation

Father God, I believe that Jesus is Your Son and that You raised Him from the dead for me. Jesus, I give my life to You. Right now, I make You the Lord of my life and choose to follow You forever. I love You and I know You love me. Thank You, Jesus, for giving me a new life. Thank You for coming into my heart and being my Savior. I am a child of God! Amen.

About the Author

For more than 15 years, Christopher Maselli has been sharing God's Word with kids through fiction. With a Master of Fine Arts in Writing, he is the author of more than 50 books, including the *Super Sleuth Investigators* mysteries, the *Amazing Laptop* series and the *Superkids Adventures.*

Chris lives in Fort Worth, Texas, with his wife and three children. His hobbies include running, collecting *"It's a Wonderful Life"* movie memorabilia and "way too much" computing.

Visit his website at ChristopherPNMaselli.com.

Other Products Available

Products Designed for Today's Children and Youth

And Jesus Healed Them All (confession book and CD gift package)
Baby Praise Board Book
Baby Praise Christmas Board Book
Load Up—A Youth Devotional
Over the Edge—A Youth Devotional
The Best of *Shout!* Adventure Comics
The *Shout!* Joke Book
The *Shout!* Super-Activity Book
Wichita Slim's Campfire Stories

*Commander Kellie and the Superkids*_{TM} Books:

Superkid Academy Children's Church Curriculum (DVD/CD curriculum)
* • Volume 1—My Father Loves Me!
* • Volume 2—The Fruit of the Spirit in You
* • Volume 3—The Sweet Life
* • Volume 4—Living in THE BLESSING
  • Volume 5—The Superkid Creed

The SWORD Adventure Book
*Commander Kellie and the Superkids*_{TM}
    Solve-It-Yourself Mysteries
*Commander Kellie and the Superkids*_{TM} Adventure Series:
    Middle Grade Novels by Christopher P.N. Maselli:

    #1 The Mysterious Presence
    #2 The Quest for the Second Half
    #3 Escape From Jungle Island
    #4 In Pursuit of the Enemy
    #5 Caged Rivalry
    #6 Mystery of the Missing Junk
    #7 Out of Breath
    #8 The Year Mashela Stole Christmas
    #9 False Identity
    #10 The Runaway Mission
    #11 The Knight-Time Rescue of Commander Kellie

*Available in Spanish

're Here for You!®

r growth in God's WORD and victory in Jesus are at the very center of hearts. In every way God has equipped us, we will help you deal with the es facing you, so you can be the **victorious overcomer** He has planned for to be.

mission of Kenneth Copeland Ministries is about all of us growing and ig together. Our prayer is that you will take full advantage of all The RD has given us to share with you.

erever you are in the world, you can watch the *Believer's Voice of Victory* adcast on television (check your local listings), the Internet cm.org or on our digital Roku channel.

r website, **kcm.org,** gives you access to every resource we've developed your victory. And, you can find contact information for our international ces in Africa, Asia, Australia, Canada, Europe, aine and our headquarters in the United States.

h office is staffed with devoted men and women, ready to serve and pray with . You can contact the worldwide office nearest you for assistance, and you can us for prayer at our U.S. number, +1-817-852-6000, 24 hours every day!

encourage you to connect with us often and let us be part of your ryday walk of faith!

s Is LORD!

Kenneth & Gloria Copeland

neth and Gloria Copeland

CPSIA information can be obtained at www.ICGtesting.com
Printed in the USA
LVOW05s2348061013

355617LV00004B/6/P